Happy Birthday Jacob
Love Uncle Mike, Aunty Audrey
Tyler + Jen

Schim Schimmel

The Family of Earth

For JoAnn, my loving champion—
this one is for you

NorthWord Press

Minnetonka, Minnesota

The world looks different to each of us.

To the gorillas, the world is a vast, green forest,
filled with trees to climb and leaves to eat.

To the lions, the world is an endless grassy plain,
sometimes hot and dry, sometimes green and wet.

Snow leopards see the world as a giant mountain, cold and windy, rocky and snowy.

Dolphins live in a world of water. Their world seems to go on forever, constantly changing from light to dark, warm to cold, shallow to deep.

Flowing rivers, quiet ponds, and muddy banks
are the only world the hippo knows.

We all live in our own worlds.

Leopards do not swim with
dolphins. They have never
seen a penguin.

Lions have never climbed the towering, windswept peaks that snow leopards call home.

And yet, all these different worlds
are the same world.

The earth may look different
to each of us, but we share only
one earth.

We share the canyons and the oceans.

We share the same sky.

We share all the forests.

In the whole universe, there is only one earth.

The earth is made from stardust.
Our bodies are made from the earth.

We are the earth come to life.

No matter where we live, all of us share
the same air, water, minerals, and plants
of this world.

The world may look
different to each of us,
but we all share the
same earth.

We are the family of earth.

Schim Schimmel describes his acrylic paintings as Environmental Visionary Surrealism. His message is that we must share this planet with all its varied life. "The central theme of my artwork and writing is the concept of planetary interdependency. I believe in an inherent unity and oneness pervading all manifested creation." Schim's artwork is reproduced in signed-and-numbered limited edition prints. His images are licensed worldwide in puzzles, school supplies, greeting cards, and other products. This is his third children's book.

© 2001 by Schim Schimmel

Edited by Judy Gitenstein
Designed by Russell S. Kuepper

NorthWord Press
5900 Green Oak Drive
Minnetonka, MN 55343
1-800-328-3895

Library of Congress Cataloging-in-Publication Data
Schimmel, Schim
    The family of Earth / author, Schim Schimmel.
        p. cm.
        Summary: All the creatures of the earth learn that though the world looks different to each of us, we are all part of the same earth.
        ISBN 1-55971-790-4 (hardcover)
        [1. Nature--Fiction.] I. Title.

PZ7.S346325 Fam 2001
[E]--dc21   2001022213

Printed in Singapore

10 9 8 7 6 5 4 3 2 1